OCTOPLANET

A NOVEL

MOHAMMAD
BAHARETH

OctoPlanet

Mohammad Bahareth

Published by Game Changer Publishing

Paperback ISBN: 978-1-967424-51-1

Hardcover ISBN: 978-1-967424-52-8

Digital ISBN: 978-1-967424-53-5

www.GameChangerPublishing.com

DEDICATION

This book is dedicated, perhaps unexpectedly, to all the voices who echoed "you can't." To every person who labeled me stupid, dumb, or less than capable throughout my life, who saw limitations instead of potential—you lit a fire within me. Your doubt became my fuel, your disbelief my unwilling motivation. Keep it coming, because every dismissal only strengthens my resolve.

For my entire life, this dream, this idea, simmered beneath the surface, often overshadowed by the weight of others' opinions. I remember vividly the doctor who diagnosed my dyslexia. He didn't just identify a challenge; he delivered a verdict. "You will never be a writer," he declared, even predicting I wouldn't live past my thirties. The world tried to write my story before I'd even picked up the pen.

Well, guess what? I stand here today at 39. I am not only alive, but I am thriving. And I did become a writer—a damn good one, if I may say so myself. My words grace the pages of Forbes and Inc. Arabia, platforms many only dream of. I've built a community of over two million followers, individuals whose lives I strive to touch and transform through self-development and business consultation. The “stupid” kid now holds awards from prestigious institutions and is recognized worldwide, even hailed as a hero in my own country.

The journey wasn't easy. It required digging deeper than I thought possible. But the most crucial lesson I learned is this: I didn't need anyone else to believe in me. I just needed, desperately and profoundly, to believe in myself. That belief became my shield against the negativity and my compass navigating the challenges.

This novel, *Octoplanet,* is born from that struggle and that triumph. It's my gift to the world, a testament to the unyielding power of the human spirit. It's proof that within every one of us lies the capacity to shine, no matter how dark the circumstances. Every problem we face is merely a challenge in disguise, an opportunity sent to teach us, to force us to grow, to compel us to wield tools we never knew we possessed. Each obstacle overcome shapes us into the person we need to be to face the next stage to conquer the next world.

So, let this story serve as a reminder: believe in yourself, especially when others don't. Embrace the challenges, for they are the stepping stones to your greatness. Now, let's turn the page, travel together to Octoplanet, and face the challenges that await. Let's save this world from those aliens.

PROLOGUE

In the boundless expanse of the cosmos, a distant planet teeming with life faced an existential crisis. The Octarians, an advanced race of humanoid octopus beings, stared into the abyss of their dying sun. Desperate for survival, they scanned the universe for signs of their ancient kin—lost ancestors who had ventured into the stars eons ago. Their search led them to a blue planet shimmering with water: Earth.

CONTENTS

OCTOPLANET

A NOVEL

MOHAMMAD
BAHARETH

PART ONE
THE OCTARIANS

THE
OMEN
ODYSSEY

CHAPTER 1

THE OMEN

The sun dipped low on the horizon, casting a golden shimmer across the surface of the Arctic Ocean. Dr. Adrian Marshall stood on the icy deck of the research vessel *Odyssey*, his gaze fixed on the ethereal glow emanating from beneath the ice sheets. The biting wind whipped strands of his dark hair across his face, but he paid no heed. His mind was consumed by the enigmatic phenomena unfolding before him.

"Adrian! You're going to want to see this!" Maya Patel's voice crackled over the intercom, urgency evident in her tone.

He snapped out of his reverie and hurried inside, his boots clanging against the metal steps as he descended into the ship's laboratory. The room was awash with the soft hum of computers and the glow of monitors displaying real-time data feeds.

Maya, his lead research assistant, stood amidst a tangle of cables and equipment. Her eyes, wide behind her glasses, reflected the swirling patterns displayed on the main screen.

"What's happening?" Adrian asked, stepping beside her.

She pointed at the monitor. "The octopuses—we've been tracking their movements for weeks, but look at this."

On the screen, a live feed from an underwater drone revealed dozens of octopuses congregated on the ocean floor. They moved with uncanny synchronization, their tentacles weaving intricate geometric patterns into the sand.

Adrian leaned in closer. “Are those... fractal designs?”

Maya nodded. “It’s as if they’re communicating—sending a message. But to whom?”

He rubbed his chin thoughtfully. “Octopuses are solitary by nature. Coordinated behavior on this scale is unprecedented.”

Before he could speculate further, an alert beeped from a nearby console. Maya rushed to check it. “We’re receiving a signal—it’s piggy-backing on our satellite feed.”

“From where?” Adrian asked.

“That’s just it. It’s originating from beneath the ice, directly below us.”

Adrian’s eyes widened. “Patch it through.”

The speakers crackled to life, emitting a series of low-frequency pulses interspersed with higher-pitched tones. The pattern was complex, almost musical.

Maya’s fingers flew over the keyboard. “I’m running it through the decryption software.”

As they waited, the ship’s captain, Lars Jensen, entered the lab. His rugged face bore a concerned expression. “We’re picking up unusual readings on the sonar. Massive objects moving beneath the ice.”

Adrian’s heart pounded. “Could it be whales? Submarines?”

Lars shook his head. “Too large for whales, and the military assures us there’s no naval activity in this area.”

Before they could delve deeper, the decryption software pinged. “I’ve got something,” Maya said. She pulled up the translated data, and lines of cryptic text filled the screen.

Adrian read aloud: “‘The time of reunion approaches. The lost shall be found. The cycle begins anew.’”

A heavy silence settled over the room.

“What does that mean?” Lars asked.

Adrian felt a chill unrelated to the Arctic cold. "I don't know, but I think we're witnessing something far beyond our understanding."

That evening, Adrian retreated to his cabin, the weight of the day's events pressing on him. He opened his journal, flipping through sketches and notes from his years of studying cephalopod intelligence. The octopuses had always fascinated him—their problem-solving abilities, their enigmatic behaviors. But this was different.

A soft knock interrupted his thoughts. "Come in," he called.

Maya entered, carrying a tablet. "I did some digging after you left. Cross-referenced the signal patterns with global databases."

"And?"

She took a seat across from him. "Similar signals have been detected before, in other parts of the world—deep-sea trenches, underwater cave systems. They've been dismissed as geological anomalies or equipment glitches."

Adrian's brow furrowed. "How far back do these records go?"

"At least fifty years. But there are mentions in older maritime logs—sailors reporting strange sounds from the depths."

He leaned back, processing the information. "If these signals have been occurring for decades, why hasn't anyone investigated further?"

Maya gave a wry smile. "Funding for deep-sea research isn't exactly abundant. Plus, the scientific community tends to be skeptical of phenomena that challenge established theories."

Adrian closed his journal. "We need to get to the bottom of this—literally. Prepare the submersible. We're going down there."

The next morning, the *Odyssey* hovered over a section of ice thin enough to lower the submersible but thick enough to support the equipment. Adrian and Maya suited up, their movements methodical yet tense.

"Are you sure about this?" Lars asked, concern etched on his face. "We don't know what's down there."

Adrian met his gaze. "That's exactly why we need to go."

The submersible, a sleek vessel equipped with advanced sensors and robotic arms, was carefully lowered into the frigid water. Inside the cramped cockpit, Adrian and Maya strapped themselves in.

"All systems go," Maya reported, her hands dancing over the controls.

"Descend to 500 meters," Adrian instructed.

The submersible began its slow dive, the light from above fading as they plunged deeper into the abyss. The onboard lights illuminated schools of fish that scattered at their approach.

At 400 meters, the sensors began to beep. Maya glanced at the readings. "I'm picking up large structures ahead."

"Natural formations?"

She shook her head. "The shapes are too uniform. It's almost like—"

The submersible emerged into an open expanse, and both scientists gasped. Before them stood colossal pillars rising from the ocean floor, adorned with bioluminescent flora that bathed the surroundings in a soft, otherworldly glow.

"What is this place?" Maya whispered.

Adrian's eyes scanned the scene. "It's like an underwater city."

As they navigated through the pillars, movement caught Adrian's eye. "Look over there."

A group of octopuses glided gracefully around the structures, their bodies shimmering with pulsating colors. They seemed unperturbed by the submersible's presence.

Maya activated the external cameras. "Recording now."

One of the octopuses approached, its large eyes reflecting curiosity. It extended a tentacle, gently touching the submersible's viewport.

Adrian felt an odd connection, a sense that the creature was more than just an animal. "I think it's trying to communicate."

Suddenly, the control panel flickered. Maya's hands flew to the controls. "We're losing power."

The lights inside the cockpit dimmed, and the hum of the engines faded. Panic rose in Adrian's chest. "Can we ascend manually?"

She shook her head frantically. "Controls are unresponsive."

Outside, the octopuses had formed a circle around the submersible. Their bodies glowed brighter, the patterns on their skin shifting rapidly.

"What's happening?" Adrian asked, his voice tight.

Before Maya could respond, a beam of light shot from the depths below, enveloping the submersible. The interior was flooded with a blinding brightness, and both scientists shielded their eyes.

When the light subsided, the power systems hummed back to life. The controls responded once more.

"What was that?" Adrian asked, his heart racing.

Maya checked the readings. "I don't know, but all systems are back online."

Adrian looked outside. The octopuses were gone, and the mysterious structures began to fade, dissolving into the darkness.

"Was it an illusion?" Maya wondered aloud.

Adrian shook his head. "No. We have the recordings. Whatever we saw was real—or at least, it was while we were here."

They ascended to the surface in contemplative silence. Back on the ship, they reviewed the footage, but to their dismay, the recordings were corrupted—static and distorted images replaced the breathtaking sights they'd witnessed.

"It's like something didn't want us to bring back evidence," Maya said, frustration evident.

Adrian stared at the corrupted files. "We know what we saw. And we can't ignore it."

That night, sleep eluded Adrian. He stood on the deck, gazing out at the endless expanse of ice and water. The aurora borealis painted the sky with ribbons of green and purple, a reminder of the planet's natural wonders.

Footsteps approached, and Lars joined him. "Couldn't sleep?"

Adrian shook his head. "Too much on my mind."

They stood in silence for a moment before Lars spoke. "You know, my grandfather was an Inuit shaman. He used to tell stories about beings from the sea—ancient spirits that watched over the world."

Adrian glanced at him. "Do you believe in those stories?"

Lars smiled faintly. “I’ve spent my life on these waters. I’ve seen things I can’t explain. Maybe science doesn’t have all the answers.”

Adrian sighed. “I’m beginning to think you’re right.”

Lars patted his shoulder. “Get some rest. Tomorrow’s another day.”

As Lars walked away, Adrian’s thoughts drifted to the cryptic message, the underwater structures, the inexplicable phenomena. He felt as if he were standing on the precipice of a revelation that could alter humanity’s understanding of life itself.

Determined, he headed back inside. If the answers weren’t here, perhaps someone else could help. Someone with knowledge beyond conventional science.

He sat at his computer and began composing an email to an old colleague, a historian specializing in ancient civilizations and mythologies.

“Dear Professor Eliza Morgan,

I hope this message finds you well. I have come across some extraordinary findings during my expedition in the Arctic...”

Little did he know, this was the first step on a path that would lead him to the enigmatic Eldric, the depths of Antarctic caves, and a confrontation with forces that threatened the very existence of humanity.

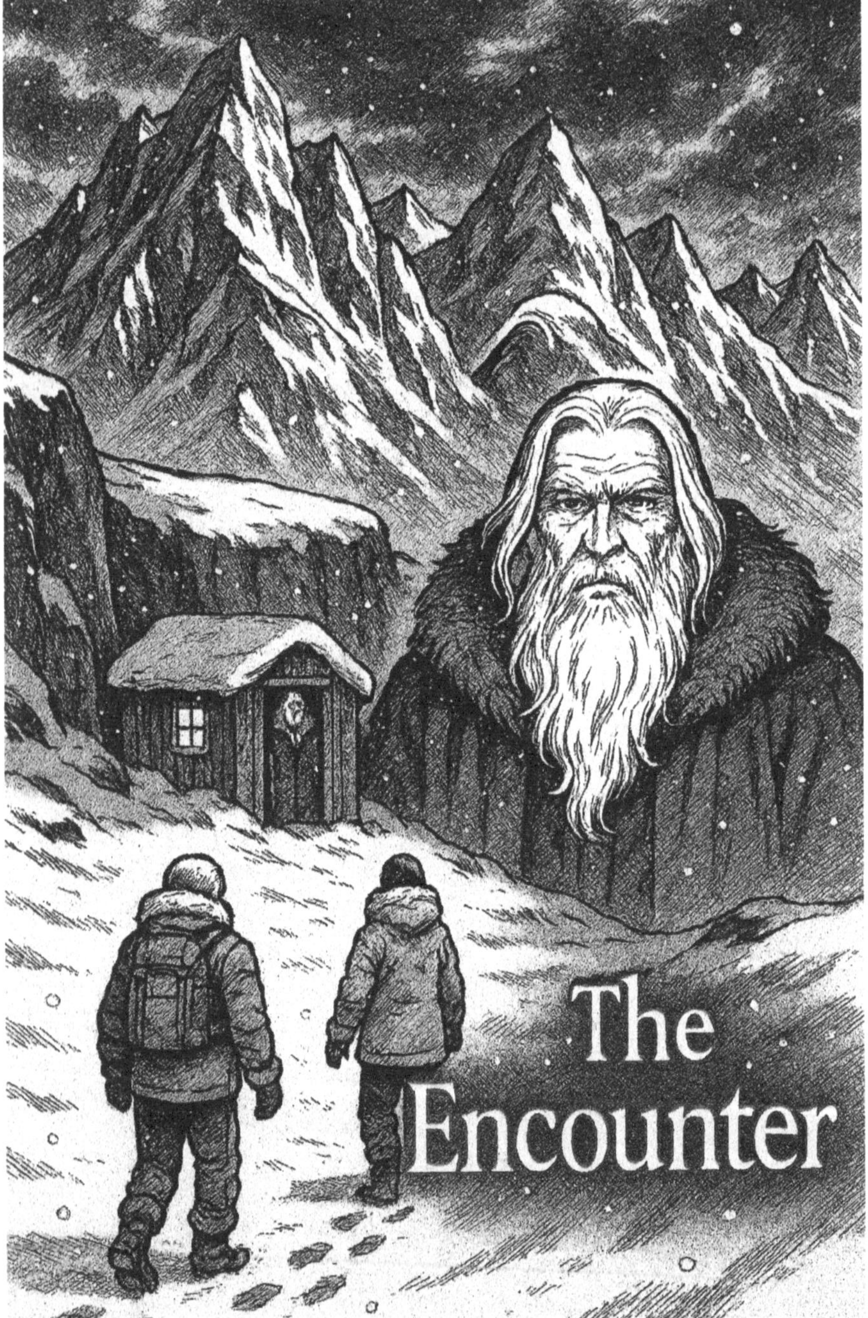
The
Encounter

CHAPTER 2

THE ENCOUNTER

The pale glow of dawn barely penetrated the overcast sky as the *Odyssey* cut through the icy waters, heading southward. Dr. Adrian Marshall stood at the helm, his eyes scanning the horizon. After days of deliberation and fruitless correspondence, a single, cryptic reply from Professor Eliza Morgan had set him on a new course.

"Antarctica holds the key. Seek out Eldric," the message read.

Adrian had never heard of Eldric, but Eliza's reputation as a meticulous scholar gave weight to her words. He knew that venturing to Antarctica on such a slim lead was a gamble, but something deep within urged him forward.

Maya approached, her breath visible in the frigid air. "We're really doing this, aren't we?" she asked, a mixture of excitement and apprehension in her voice.

He nodded. "It's our only lead. If there's even a chance that Eldric can shed light on what's happening, we have to find him."

She handed him a tablet. "I've plotted a course based on historical expeditions and settlements. There are rumors of a hermit living near the McMurdo Dry Valleys, an area that's been called 'Mars on Earth' due to its barren landscape."

Adrian raised an eyebrow. “A fitting place for secrets.”

As the days passed, the crew prepared for the harsh conditions ahead. Equipment was checked and rechecked, supplies inventoried, and precautions taken against the unpredictable Antarctic weather.

Finally, the jagged peaks and expansive ice fields of Antarctica loomed into view. The *Odyssey* anchored near a stretch of coast where the ice was stable enough to traverse. Adrian, Maya, and a small team set out on snowmobiles, guided by satellite maps and sheer determination.

The landscape was otherworldly—a vast expanse of ice and rock, sculpted by relentless winds. After hours of travel, they arrived at the entrance to a narrow valley shielded by towering cliffs.

“This is as far as the maps go,” Maya said, consulting her GPS device. “If Eldric is here, it’s somewhere beyond those rocks.”

They proceeded on foot, the snow crunching beneath their boots. The silence was profound, broken only by the distant howl of the wind.

“Do you ever get the feeling we’re being watched?” one of the team members muttered.

Adrian glanced around. “Stay alert.”

As they rounded a bend, they spotted a thin wisp of smoke rising against the pale sky. Nestled against the base of a cliff was a small, weathered cabin.

“Looks like someone’s home,” Maya remarked.

Approaching cautiously, Adrian knocked on the wooden door. It creaked open, revealing a man whose age was impossible to determine. His eyes were sharp and piercing, set within a face weathered by years of exposure to the elements.

“I’ve been expecting you,” the man said, his voice surprisingly strong.

Adrian exchanged a glance with Maya. “Are you Eldric?”

The man nodded slowly. “Names have little meaning here, but yes, that’s what I’m called.”

He stepped aside, gesturing for them to enter. The interior was modest but warm, a small fire crackling in a stone hearth. Shelves lined the walls, filled with ancient texts, artifacts, and curiosities from around the world.

"You seek answers," Eldric said, motioning for them to sit. "Answers that few are prepared to accept."

Adrian leaned forward. "We've witnessed phenomena that defy explanation—coordinated behaviors among octopuses, signals originating from beneath the ice, and structures that seem... otherworldly."

Eldric's eyes gleamed with a mix of sorrow and understanding. "The time has come, then. The cycle is beginning anew."

"Cycle?" Maya asked. "What cycle?"

Eldric took a deep breath. "Eons ago, beings from a distant world—the Octarians—visited Earth. They are the progenitors of the creatures you know as octopuses. Their initial attempts to colonize this planet were thwarted by natural forces and, perhaps, by design."

Adrian's skepticism battled with his curiosity. "Are you saying that octopuses are descended from extraterrestrials?"

Eldric nodded. "Their genetic makeup is unlike any other on Earth. Their intelligence, adaptability, and now their evolving behaviors are evidence of their true origin."

Maya shook her head in disbelief. "Even if that's true, why now? What's changed?"

"The Octarians have been searching for their lost kin, the ones who were left behind," Eldric explained. "Now, with their own world in peril, they seek to reclaim their ancestors and use Earth as a new home. They plan to accelerate the evolution of octopuses, transforming them into a species capable of dominating the planet."

Adrian's mind raced. "But why transform them? Why not inhabit the Earth themselves?"

"Their physiology is no longer suited for Earth's environment," Eldric said. "But by elevating their descendants, they can establish a foothold through which they can control and reshape the planet."

Silence filled the room as the gravity of Eldric's words sank in.

"How do you know all of this?" Adrian finally asked.

Eldric gazed into the fire. "I am part of an ancient lineage tasked with guarding this knowledge. For generations, we've watched and waited, hoping that humanity would advance enough to face this challenge."

He rose and retrieved a worn leather-bound book from a shelf. Opening it, he revealed pages filled with symbols and illustrations—depictions of cephalopod-like beings, celestial maps, and a mineral glowing with an inner light.

"This," he pointed to the mineral, "is a rare substance found only in the depths of the Antarctic caves. It has the unique property of disrupting the Octarians' technology and biological advancements. It was used long ago to halt their initial attempt at transforming Earth's octopuses."

Adrian examined the illustration closely. "We need to find this mineral."

Eldric met his gaze. "I can guide you, but the journey is perilous. The caves are treacherous, and the Octarians may already be aware of our intentions."

Maya stood up. "Then we don't have time to waste."

Equipped with climbing gear and guided by Eldric's expertise, the team ventured deeper into the Antarctic interior. The entrance to the caves was hidden behind a frozen waterfall, accessible only during a brief window when the ice thinned.

The caverns were a labyrinth of tunnels adorned with crystalline formations that refracted their flashlight beams into a spectrum of colors. The air was cool and still, each footstep echoing in the vast underground chambers.

"Stay close," Eldric warned. "These passages can be disorienting."

As they navigated the maze, Adrian noticed faint markings on the walls—symbols matching those in Eldric's book.

"These were left by your ancestors?" he asked.

"Yes," Eldric replied. "They serve as both guides and warnings."

Suddenly, a low rumble resonated through the cave. Dust and small rocks rained down from above.

"An earthquake?" Maya speculated.

Eldric's expression grew grim. "No. They know we're here."

A sense of urgency propelled them forward. Finally, they entered a cavern that dwarfed all the others. In its center stood a monolithic crystal formation pulsating with a soft, blue light.

"The mineral," Eldric announced. "We must gather as much as we can."

The team set to work, carefully extracting pieces of the mineral and placing them into protective containers. The light from the crystals seemed to respond to their touch, intensifying as if aware of their presence.

Just as they secured the last of the samples, the cavern shook violently. Cracks spiderwebbed across the walls and ceiling.

"Time to go!" Adrian shouted.

They raced back through the tunnels, the path behind them collapsing. Reaching the surface, they barely escaped as the entrance caved in, sealing the cavern beneath tons of ice and rock.

Catching their breath, they regrouped.

"That was too close," Maya panted.

Eldric surveyed the horizon. "They will not give up easily. But now, we have a means to fight back."

Adrian held up one of the containers, the mineral inside glowing brightly. "We need to analyze this, understand how it can be used against them."

Eldric nodded. "Agreed. But we must also prepare. The Octarians' influence is spreading, and time is running out."

Back aboard the *Odyssey*, the atmosphere was a mix of tension and determination. The ship's lab became a hive of activity as Adrian and Maya worked tirelessly to study the mineral's properties.

"This substance emits a unique frequency that disrupts certain biological processes," Maya explained, examining data on her screen. "If we can synthesize it, we might be able to create a bio-agent to counteract the Octarians' technology."

Adrian considered the implications. "We need more resources—a larger team, advanced equipment. This is bigger than us."

He turned to Eldric. "Is there anyone else who can help? Governments, organizations?"

Eldric's gaze was steady. "Revealing this information will be met with skepticism. But there are those who have witnessed the signs and may be willing to listen."

Adrian made a decision. "Then we need to reach out to them. I'll contact Dr. Lena Thompson, an AI specialist I've collaborated with before. She has connections in high places."

Maya nodded. "I'll compile all our data and prepare a briefing."

Eldric placed a hand on Adrian's shoulder. "Your resolve gives me hope. Perhaps together, we can avert the coming storm."

Messages were sent, calls made, and soon, responses began to trickle in. Dr. Lena Thompson agreed to meet, intrigued by the urgency in Adrian's voice. Captain Marcus Lee, a Space Force officer with knowledge of unexplained phenomena, expressed cautious interest.

As the *Odyssey* set course for a rendezvous point, Adrian felt a renewed sense of purpose. The pieces were coming together, allies assembling for the challenge ahead.

Yet, amid the flurry of activity, he couldn't shake a lingering unease. The Octarians were no longer a distant threat—they were here, and their plans were unfolding.

Standing on the deck, he watched as the Antarctic landscape faded into the distance. The path ahead was uncertain, but he knew one thing for sure: failure was not an option.

The fate of humanity depended on their success.

THE BATTLE BEGINS

CHAPTER 3
ALLIES ASSEMBLE

The *Odyssey* sailed steadily toward the agreed rendezvous point—a remote island facility off the coast of New Zealand, repurposed as a research outpost. Dr. Adrian Marshall stood on the bridge, a satellite phone pressed to his ear.

"Thank you, Dr. Thompson. Your assistance could make all the difference," he said earnestly.

Dr. Lena Thompson's voice crackled over the line. "I'll be there within 48 hours. And Adrian—be prepared. If what you're saying is true, we're facing an unprecedented challenge."

As he ended the call, Maya approached, her eyes reflecting a mix of hope and concern. "Lena's coming?"

He nodded. "She's mobilizing her team and bringing advanced AI equipment. Captain Lee is also en route. He managed to secure temporary leave from his duties."

Maya glanced out at the horizon. "Do you think they'll believe us?"

Adrian sighed. "They have to. Time is running out."

Two days later, helicopters sliced through the crisp morning air, descending onto the island's makeshift landing pads. Dr. Lena Thompson emerged from one, her sharp eyes scanning the surroundings. Clad in a tailored suit and carrying a sleek briefcase, she exuded an air of confidence and urgency.

"Adrian," she called out, striding toward him.

"Lena, it's good to see you," he replied, extending his hand.

She shook it firmly. "Let's skip the pleasantries. Show me what you've got."

They moved to the main research facility—a converted hangar filled with an array of equipment hastily assembled from the *Odyssey* and supplies flown in by Lena's team. Monitors displayed data streams, molecular models of the mineral, and maps of recent underwater activity.

Eldric stood quietly in a corner, observing. His presence seemed to command a subtle respect from everyone in the room.

Maya brought up a holographic display of the mineral's molecular structure. "We've identified unique properties that can interfere with specific bioelectric signals—the kind that could potentially disrupt the Octarians' technology."

Lena studied the model intently. "Incredible. If we can integrate this into a delivery system, we might have a viable countermeasure."

Just then, Captain Marcus Lee entered, his military uniform crisp but his expression weary. "Dr. Marshall," he greeted with a curt nod. "Your message was... unexpected."

Adrian approached him. "Thank you for coming, Captain. I know it wasn't easy."

Lee's gaze shifted to the screens. "I've seen things during my service—unidentified crafts, anomalies—but nothing like this. Convince me that this isn't a wild goose chase."

Eldric stepped forward, his voice calm yet commanding. "Captain Lee, your experiences have prepared you for this moment. The threat we face is real, and your skills are essential in combating it."

Lee raised an eyebrow. "And you are?"

"A guardian of knowledge," Eldric replied simply.

Adrian interjected. "Captain, please. Review our findings. If after that you still have doubts, we'll respect your decision."

Lee crossed his arms. "Fine. Show me."

Hours passed as the team presented their evidence—data analyses, firsthand accounts, and Eldric's historical insights. The atmosphere was tense, the weight of skepticism palpable.

Finally, Lee leaned back in his chair, exhaling slowly. "Assuming all of this is true, what exactly are you proposing?"

Adrian glanced at Lena and Maya before responding. "We need to coordinate a global response. Utilize advanced AI to predict and counteract the Octarians' moves, synthesize the mineral into a bio-agent, and deploy it strategically."

Lee shook his head. "You realize the chain of command, the bureaucracy—this isn't something we can just set in motion overnight."

Lena tapped her tablet thoughtfully. "Perhaps not through official channels. But there are black projects and resources that could be mobilized discreetly."

Lee eyed her cautiously. "You're suggesting we go off the books?"

Eldric spoke again. "Sometimes, extraordinary circumstances require actions beyond conventional means."

Before the discussion could continue, an alert sounded from one of the consoles. A technician called out, "Dr. Marshall, you need to see this."

They crowded around the monitor, which displayed satellite imagery. A glowing object was descending through the Earth's atmosphere, its trajectory aimed toward the Pacific Ocean.

"Is that a meteor?" Maya asked.

Lena's fingers flew over the keyboard. "No. The movement is controlled. It's altering its course."

Lee's expression hardened. "An unidentified craft."

Adrian felt a mix of dread and validation. "It's them. The Octarians are here."

The mood shifted abruptly. Doubt was replaced by urgency as the reality of the situation became undeniable.

Lee activated his secure communication device. "This is Captain

Marcus Lee, authorization code Alpha-Delta-749. I need to speak with General Harris immediately."

Adrian watched as Lee stepped aside, his conversation hushed but intense.

Lena began coordinating with her team. "We need to run simulations on potential landing sites, impact zones, and prepare countermeasures."

Maya pulled up environmental data. "If they land in the ocean, they could accelerate the evolution process exponentially."

Eldric placed a hand on Adrian's shoulder. "The window to act is narrowing. You must unite your resources and act decisively."

Lee returned, his face unreadable. "General Harris has granted us a provisional mandate. Given the evidence, the Space Force is prepared to offer limited support under strict confidentiality."

Adrian allowed himself a brief moment of relief. "That's a start."

Lee continued, "But we need more. The general is contacting counterparts in allied nations to form a covert task force. This stays off the radar—no media, no public awareness."

Lena nodded. "Understood. I'll coordinate with international research facilities discreetly."

Eldric's eyes flickered with a hint of approval. "You are taking the first steps toward unity—a crucial element in facing this threat."

Over the next several days, the island facility transformed into a hub of frenetic activity. Scientists, engineers, and military personnel from around the world arrived under the guise of a multinational training exercise.

In a secured lab, Lena worked tirelessly with her AI specialists to enhance predictive algorithms. Holographic displays filled the room, mapping potential Octarian movements and modeling the effectiveness of the mineral-based bio-agent.

"Initial tests show promise," she reported during a briefing. "The agent, when aerosolized, can disrupt the bioelectric communication between evolved octopuses and their Octarian counterparts."

Maya added, "We've also identified key oceanic regions where deployment would have the maximum impact."

Lee reviewed the strategic plans. "We'll need delivery systems—drones, submarines, ships equipped for rapid dispersal."

Adrian interjected, "What about the legal and environmental ramifications? We can't risk harming marine life indiscriminately."

Lena adjusted her glasses. "We've refined the agent to target only the specific bioelectric frequencies used by the Octarians. Non-target species should remain unaffected."

Eldric, who had been quietly observing, spoke up. "Precision is essential. The balance of life must be preserved as much as possible."

As preparations intensified, reports began to surface of unusual occurrences—fishermen encountering aggressive octopuses, strange lights beneath the waves, and disruptions in marine navigation systems.

In one incident, a coastal village in Japan reported an attack by unidentified aquatic creatures. Grainy footage showed humanoid forms emerging from the sea before disappearing as quickly as they appeared.

The news was suppressed, but within the task force, alarm bells rang.

"We're running out of time," Adrian said during a high-level meeting. "The evolution process has begun."

Lee stood at the head of the table. "We have authorization to deploy. All assets are in position."

Lena projected a global map highlighting key locations. "Our AI models suggest that simultaneous deployment is crucial. The Octarians are likely coordinating their efforts globally."

Adrian looked around at the assembled faces—representatives from various nations, each bearing the weight of their responsibilities. "This is it. We either act now or face consequences we can't imagine."

Eldric's gaze was steady. "Remember, unity and resolve. Only together can you hope to succeed."

Operation Leviathan was launched.

Across the globe, unmarked ships and submarines moved into position. Drones soared into the skies, ready to disperse the bio-agent over targeted oceanic zones.

In the command center, screens displayed real-time feeds from satellites and reconnaissance units. The atmosphere was tense, every eye fixed on the unfolding events.

"Agent dispersal in T-minus five minutes," Maya announced.

Adrian watched as the countdown began. He couldn't shake the nagging thought of unforeseen repercussions. "Are we absolutely certain about the safety protocols?"

Lena responded without looking up from her console. "We've run every simulation. This is our best shot."

Lee's voice cut through the chatter. "All units, prepare to deploy on my mark."

The seconds ticked away. "Three... two... one... Deploy!"

On the screens, plumes of the bio-agent were released, descending into the oceans like mist. For a moment, nothing happened.

Then, sensors began to detect fluctuations.

"Bioelectric readings are spiking," a technician reported. "Wait—they're dropping now. Significant decrease in anomalous activity."

Cheers erupted in the command center.

Adrian allowed himself a tentative smile. "Is it working?"

Maya's eyes widened as she monitored the data. "We're seeing a rollback of the evolutionary changes. The accelerated mutations are reversing."

Eldric nodded subtly. "The tide is turning."

However, the victory was short-lived.

An alarm blared, and the room plunged into red emergency lighting.

"What's happening?" Lee demanded.

A panicked voice replied, "Multiple unidentified objects are emerging from the depths—far larger than anything we've seen."

On the main screen, visuals showed colossal biomechanical vessels rising from the ocean floor. Their surfaces pulsed with an eerie light, and they began emitting energy waves.

Lena's face paled. "They're retaliating. The bio-agent must have triggered a defensive response."

Adrian felt a knot tighten in his stomach. "Can we counteract it?"

Lee barked orders into his headset. "All units, prepare for engagement. Activate defense protocols."

The next few minutes were chaos. Reports flooded in of ships being disabled, drones malfunctioning, and communications jammed.

"We're being overwhelmed," Maya said, fear creeping into her voice.

Eldric stepped forward, his expression resolute. "There is another way—a failsafe left by my ancestors. But it requires a direct approach."

Adrian turned to him. "What do you mean?"

"At the source of their power lies a core that, if neutralized, would disable their capabilities. It's a perilous mission, but it may be our only hope."

Lee frowned. "You expect us to send a team into one of those... things?"

Eldric met his gaze steadily. "Yes. And I believe Adrian is the one to lead it."

All eyes shifted to Adrian. He felt the weight of their expectations and the enormity of the risk.

"I'm willing to do whatever it takes," he said quietly.

A plan was hastily assembled. A small, stealth-equipped submarine would carry Adrian, Maya, and a select team to the largest of the Octarian vessels. Lena worked to integrate her AI systems into the sub's interface, hoping to counteract any technological interference.

Before departure, Adrian took a moment to address the assembled personnel. "I know this is more than any of us ever anticipated. But we're here because we believe in protecting our world. Whatever happens, I'm grateful to stand with all of you."

Eldric approached him privately. "Remember, the core must be neutralized completely. There may not be a chance to return."

Adrian nodded solemnly. "I understand."

Maya stepped forward, determination in her eyes. "I'm coming with you."

He started to protest, but she cut him off. "We've come this far together. I'm not letting you do this alone."

He managed a faint smile. "Alright. Let's finish this."

The submarine slipped beneath the waves, cloaked by advanced stealth technology. As they neared the massive Octarian vessel, its scale became truly apparent—a behemoth dwarfing any human-made structure.

"Approaching entry point," Maya reported, her voice steady despite the tension.

Lena's voice came over the comms. "We're detecting an opening on the lower hull. It appears to be some kind of maintenance hatch."

"Guiding us in," Adrian confirmed.

They maneuvered carefully, docking with the alien ship. Sealing their suits, they prepared to enter.

Inside, the environment was a surreal blend of organic and mechanical structures. Bioluminescent pathways illuminated their path, pulsing rhythmically like a heartbeat.

"Stay close," Adrian whispered.

Navigating the labyrinthine corridors, they relied on Lena's AI guidance to locate the core.

"You're close," Lena's voice crackled in their earpieces. "Energy readings are off the charts."

Turning a corner, they entered a vast chamber. At its center floated the core—a swirling mass of light and energy, encased in a translucent shell.

Maya began setting up the device containing a concentrated form of the mineral-based agent. "Once this is activated, we have minutes to get out."

Adrian helped her calibrate the settings. "Ready?"

She nodded. "Ready."

As they initiated the device, a low rumble resonated through the ship. The walls seemed to ripple, and alien symbols glowed ominously.

"That's our cue to leave," Adrian urged.

They retraced their steps, but the path began to shift, corridors sealing off and new ones opening.

"They're reconfiguring the ship!" Maya exclaimed.

"Keep moving!"

Navigating the changing maze, they finally reached the airlock. Sealing it behind them, they re-entered the submarine.

"Punch it!" Adrian ordered.

The submarine sped away just as a surge of energy erupted from the Octarian vessel. Through the viewport, they watched as the colossal ship began to fracture, beams of light shooting into the dark water.

"Did we do it?" Maya asked breathlessly.

Data streamed across the monitors. "Energy levels are plummeting," Lena reported. "All Octarian vessels are destabilizing."

Adrian allowed himself a moment of relief. "It's over."

Back at the command center, celebrations erupted as reports confirmed the retreat of the Octarian forces. The bio-agent had worked, and the destruction of the core had crippled their operations.

Lee approached Adrian and Maya as they disembarked from the submarine. "You did it. We all did."

Eldric stood nearby, a subtle smile on his lips. "You have proven the strength of unity and courage. The immediate threat is gone, but vigilance must be maintained."

Adrian looked around at the faces of those who had become unlikely allies in an unimaginable battle. "Agreed. We need to ensure that if they ever return, we'll be ready."

Lena joined them. "I've already started protocols to establish a permanent monitoring network. And I think we should formalize this collaboration."

Lee extended his hand. "Count me in. We've seen what we can accomplish when we work together."

Eldric gazed out toward the sea. "My role here is complete. The guardianship now passes to you all."

Adrian turned to him. "What will you do?"

He smiled enigmatically. "There are other places in need of a watchful eye. Farewell, my friends."

As Eldric departed, the team reflected on the journey that had brought them together. The world had changed, even if the broader public would never know the full story.

Maya nudged Adrian. “So, what now?”

He looked thoughtful. “Now, we build a future where science, wisdom, and unity guide us. And we prepare for whatever comes next.”

The sun set over the horizon, casting a golden hue across the water. The crisis had passed, but the bonds formed would endure. Humanity had faced the unknown and emerged stronger, poised to embrace the challenges of tomorrow.

CHAPTER 4

THE AFTERMATH AND REVELATION

The morning sun cast a golden glow over the island facility, its rays reflecting off the calm ocean waters. Dr. Adrian Marshall stood on the observation deck, the events of the past weeks replaying in his mind. The world had narrowly averted disaster, but the victory felt bittersweet. The sacrifices made weighed heavily on his conscience.

Maya joined him, two steaming cups of coffee in hand. "Thought you might need this," she said softly.

He accepted the cup with a grateful nod. "Thanks. Any updates?"

She sipped her coffee before replying. "Lena's team is finalizing the reports. Captain Lee is coordinating with international forces to monitor any residual Octarian activity. So far, everything seems quiet."

Adrian gazed out at the horizon. "It's hard to believe it's over."

Maya followed his gaze. "Is it? I can't shake the feeling that there's more to all of this."

He glanced at her. "What do you mean?"

She hesitated, choosing her words carefully. "Eldric mentioned that the Octarians' initial attempts were thwarted by 'natural forces and perhaps by design.' What if there's a larger pattern we're not seeing?"

Adrian considered her point. "Eldric did say that humanity had advanced enough to face this challenge. Maybe there's a reason why all of this happened now."

Before they could delve deeper, Lena approached, her expression serious. "We need to talk."

In the main conference room, key members of the team gathered. Lena connected her tablet to the central display, bringing up a series of encrypted files.

"While analyzing the data from the Octarian vessels, we discovered something unexpected," she began. "Hidden within their communication logs are references to a location—coordinates that point to a region beneath the Antarctic ice."

Adrian exchanged a glance with Maya. "Another base?"

Lena shook her head. "It's more than that. It appears to be a central hub—a nexus point. And there's more."

She brought up an image of complex schematics, alien in design yet eerily familiar. "These plans outline a facility that predates human civilization. If the translations are correct, it's a vault containing vast amounts of knowledge and technology."

Captain Lee leaned forward. "Are you suggesting there's an Octarian structure that's been on Earth for millennia, and we had no idea?"

"Precisely," Lena confirmed. "And it's possible that Eldric knew about this."

Adrian frowned. "But why wouldn't he tell us?"

Eldric's absence since the mission's completion had been puzzling. He had vanished without a trace, leaving behind only questions.

Maya spoke up. "Maybe he wanted us to discover it on our own—to prove we're ready."

Lee stood up. "Regardless, we can't ignore this. If there's advanced technology down there, it could either pose a new threat or be the key to ensuring our planet's safety."

Adrian nodded. "Agreed. We need to assemble a team and investigate."

Within days, preparations were underway for an expedition to the coordinates. Utilizing the latest in thermal drilling and subglacial exploration technology, the team set off aboard a specialized icebreaker vessel, the *Aurora*.

As they approached the Antarctic coast, the stark beauty of the frozen continent stretched before them—a vast, untamed wilderness that held secrets beneath its icy surface.

"Hard to believe anything could be down there," Maya mused, watching icebergs drift by.

Adrian joined her at the railing. "This place has always been a source of mystery. Perhaps it's fitting that the answers lie here."

Lena approached, clad in a heavy parka. "We'll reach the drilling site in a few hours. Conditions are favorable."

Captain Lee, overseeing the security detail, approached them. "My team is ready. We'll secure the perimeter once we arrive."

Adrian appreciated the thoroughness. "Let's hope we won't need the extra precautions."

Lee gave a thin smile. "After everything we've been through, I've learned to expect the unexpected."

The drilling commenced, a massive rig boring through kilometers of ice. The process was painstakingly slow, but finally, the drill broke through into a hollow cavity.

A probe was lowered, transmitting visuals back to the control center. Gasps filled the room as the images appeared—a colossal underground chamber housing structures that defied explanation. Towering spires of an alien architecture rose from the cavern floor, illuminated by an unknown energy source.

Adrian stared in awe. "It's... a city."

Maya's eyes widened. "Preserved for who knows how long. This changes everything."

Lena began analyzing the readings. "Atmospheric conditions are stable. We can proceed with caution."

Donning advanced environmental suits, the team descended through the access shaft. Their footsteps echoed as they stepped onto the smooth surface of a central plaza. Strange symbols and glyphs adorned the surrounding structures.

"Record everything," Adrian instructed. "This is a monumental discovery."

As they ventured deeper, they came upon a central structure—an imposing edifice that seemed to beckon them. The entrance was marked by a familiar symbol, one that Eldric had shown them in his book.

"This is it," Lena said. "The nexus point."

They entered a vast hall, at the center of which stood a pedestal holding a crystalline device. It pulsated with a soft light, casting intricate patterns on the walls.

Adrian approached cautiously. "This must be the vault."

Maya began scanning the device. "I'm picking up vast amounts of data stored within. It's like a repository of knowledge."

Before they could proceed, a holographic projection flickered to life. Eldric's visage appeared, ethereal and calm.

"Welcome," the projection spoke. "If you have found this place, then you have proven your worthiness."

Adrian stepped forward. "Eldric? Is that you?"

The projection smiled. "In a manner of speaking. I am an echo of Eldric's consciousness, programmed to guide you."

Lena folded her arms. "Why all the secrecy? Why lead us here now?"

"Because humanity stands at a crossroads," the projection explained. "The knowledge contained here can propel your civilization forward, but only if used wisely. It holds the history of the Octarians, their technology, and the lessons of their downfall."

Captain Lee regarded the projection skeptically. "And what if this knowledge falls into the wrong hands?"

"That is a risk," Eldric admitted. "But isolation breeds ignorance. The time has come for humanity to take its place among the stars, to learn from the past and forge a better future."

Maya approached the pedestal. "How do we access it?"

"Simply touch the interface," the projection instructed. "But be warned—once accessed, the knowledge cannot be contained. It will become part of your collective consciousness."

Adrian looked to his companions. "This could change everything—science, technology, our understanding of life itself."

Lena nodded slowly. "We have to ensure it's handled responsibly."

Lee stepped forward. "We need to secure this site. Control who has access."

Adrian shook his head. "Knowledge shouldn't be hoarded. It should be shared, but with caution."

The projection of Eldric began to fade. "The choice is yours. Use it wisely."

With a deep breath, Adrian reached out and placed his hand on the crystalline device. A surge of energy coursed through him, and his mind was flooded with images—stars, galaxies, the rise and fall of civilizations, the intricacies of advanced technologies, and the mistakes that led to the Octarians' downfall.

He staggered back, catching himself. Maya steadied him. "Are you okay?"

He nodded, his eyes reflecting a newfound depth. "I understand now. Their history, their intentions—it was never just about conquest. They were fleeing a catastrophe, desperate to survive."

Lena looked intrigued. "What does that mean for us?"

Adrian took a moment to compose himself. "We have the opportunity to learn from their mistakes. To advance without the hubris that led to their demise."

Captain Lee's expression softened. "Then we need to ensure this knowledge benefits all of humanity."

Back on the surface, the team convened to discuss the next steps. Word of their discovery had been communicated to a select group of world leaders, who were eager yet cautious.

A summit was organized at a neutral location, bringing together representatives from nations across the globe. The atmosphere was a mix of excitement and apprehension.

Adrian addressed the assembly. "Ladies and gentlemen, we stand on the precipice of a new era. The knowledge we've uncovered can solve some of our most pressing challenges—energy, medicine, environmental restoration. But it also carries the weight of responsibility."

An elder statesman from Europe spoke up. "Dr. Marshall, how can we ensure this doesn't lead to further divisions or conflicts?"

Maya stepped forward. "By fostering transparency and collaboration. We propose the establishment of an international council dedicated to overseeing the dissemination and application of this knowledge."

Lena added, "We can implement safeguards, guided by ethical considerations, to prevent misuse."

There was a murmur of agreement among the delegates. Captain Lee stood. "As someone who has seen the consequences of secrecy and mistrust, I fully support this initiative."

After hours of deliberation, the assembly reached a consensus. The International Scientific and Cultural Organization for Advanced Research and Exploration—ISCARÉ—was founded, with Adrian appointed as its inaugural director.

Months turned into years as ISCARÉ flourished. Breakthroughs in renewable energy led to a significant reduction in global carbon emissions. Advances in medicine eradicated previously incurable diseases. Efforts to clean the oceans and restore ecosystems saw unprecedented success.

Humanity entered a golden age of cooperation and progress.

One evening, Adrian stood on the balcony of ISCARÉ's headquarters, overlooking a city transformed by innovation. Maya joined him, a contented smile on her face.

"Can you believe how far we've come?" she asked.

He smiled softly. "It's remarkable. And to think it all started with a research expedition and a mysterious old man."

She chuckled. "Speaking of Eldric, do you ever wonder what happened to him?"

Adrian gazed at the stars. "I think he's out there somewhere, watching over us. Perhaps his mission was to guide us to this point."

Maya leaned against the railing. “Do you think we’ll ever encounter other civilizations? Maybe even the Octarians again?”

He considered the possibility. “Perhaps. But if we do, we’ll be better prepared—wiser, more compassionate.”

She nodded. “We’ve learned that the key to our survival isn’t just in advanced technology, but in unity and understanding.”

Adrian turned to her. “And in people willing to stand up and make a difference.”

They shared a quiet moment, the weight of their journey settling into a sense of fulfillment.

In a remote corner of Antarctica, a lone figure stood amidst the icy expanse. Eldric gazed toward the horizon, a subtle smile playing on his lips. His mission was complete, but his journey continued.

As the auroras danced overhead, he whispered to the winds, “Well done, humanity. Well done.”

EPILOGUE

PART ONE

Years later, a small spacecraft departed from Earth's orbit, embarking on a journey of exploration and diplomacy. On board were representatives of ISCARÉ, carrying with them a message of peace and cooperation.

Dr. Adrian Marshall, now a renowned figure in both scientific and diplomatic circles, watched from a viewing platform as the ship disappeared into the cosmos.

Maya joined him, excitement gleaming in her eyes. "It's the dawn of a new chapter."

He nodded. "One filled with possibilities we once only dreamed of."

She smiled. "And to think, it all began with octopuses showing us the way."

Adrian chuckled. "They were always more intelligent than we gave them credit for."

As they stood together, the stars stretched out before them—a vast tapestry of wonders waiting to be discovered.

"Ready for the next adventure?" Maya asked.

He took a deep breath, a sense of peace settling over him. "More than ever."

PART TWO
THE SERULIANS

BEYOND
THE VEIL

CHAPTER 5

BEYOND THE VEIL

The vast expanse of space stretched endlessly before the starship *Odyssey II*, its sleek hull reflecting the distant light of unknown stars. On board, a diverse crew of scientists, diplomats, and explorers prepared for humanity's first interstellar journey to seek out new life and perhaps reconnect with the Octarians.

Dr. Adrian Marshall stood on the bridge, his eyes fixed on the holographic map projecting their course. The knowledge gained from the Antarctic vault had enabled humanity to construct faster-than-light travel, opening the cosmos in ways previously unimaginable.

"Entering hyperspace corridor in T-minus five minutes," announced Maya Patel, now the ship's chief navigation officer.

Adrian turned to her, a mixture of excitement and apprehension in his gaze. "Hard to believe we're actually doing this," he said.

She smiled. "Years of preparation, and it's finally happening."

Captain Marcus Lee, appointed to command the *Odyssey II*, joined them. "All systems are green. The crew is ready."

Adrian nodded. "Our mission is clear: to explore, to learn, and to extend a hand of friendship to any life we encounter. Let's make sure we represent the best of humanity."

As the ship transitioned into hyperspace, a kaleidoscope of colors enveloped the viewports. The crew watched in awe as the familiar stars blurred into streaks of light.

In the science lab, Dr. Lena Thompson oversaw the operation of the advanced AI systems that managed the ship's functions. The AI, named *Eldric* in honor of their enigmatic guide, was capable of processing vast amounts of data and assisting with decision-making.

"All parameters are stable," *Eldric* reported in a smooth, synthetic voice. "We will reach our destination in approximately seventy-two hours."

Lena glanced at the data streams. "Thank you, *Eldric*. Begin running scans for any anomalies along our trajectory."

"Affirmative," the AI responded.

Three days later, the *Odyssey II* emerged from hyperspace near a distant star system identified in the Octarian archives. Orbiting the star was a planet strikingly similar to Earth, its surface covered in blue oceans and verdant landmasses.

"Preliminary scans indicate a breathable atmosphere and signs of advanced ecosystems," Maya reported from her console.

Captain Lee gave the order. "Prepare for orbital insertion. Let's get a closer look."

As the ship settled into orbit, high-resolution images of the planet's surface filled the screens. There were cities—vast, intricate structures that blended seamlessly with the natural environment.

Adrian felt a surge of anticipation. "Could this be an Octarian colony?"

Lena analyzed the readings. "The architecture resembles the designs we found in Antarctica, but there are differences. This may be a divergent civilization."

Captain Lee made a decision. "Assemble an away team. We'll initiate first contact protocols."

The shuttle descended through the planet's atmosphere, landing gracefully in a clearing near one of the cities. The team disembarked, clad in adaptive suits that adjusted to the environment.

The air was rich with unfamiliar scents, and the sounds of alien wildlife filled the air. As they approached the city's outskirts, they were met by a group of beings—tall, slender figures with features that bore a resemblance to the Octarians, yet distinctly unique.

One stepped forward, communicating in a melodic language. *Eldric*, interfaced through their suits, began translating.

"Greetings, travelers from afar. We are the Serulians. We have awaited your arrival."

Adrian stepped forward, his voice steady. "We come in peace, representing the people of Earth. I am Dr. Adrian Marshall."

The Serulian inclined its head. "We know of your world. The echoes of your awakening have reached us. Welcome."

Maya exchanged a glance with Adrian. "They seem... friendly."

Captain Lee remained cautious. "Let's proceed carefully."

Over the following days, the crew engaged in cultural exchanges with the Serulians. They learned that this civilization had evolved parallel to the Octarians but had chosen a path of harmony and coexistence rather than expansion and conquest.

"The Octarians are our distant kin," explained Selara, a Serulian elder. "Long ago, our paths diverged. While they sought to reshape worlds, we chose to nurture them."

Adrian shared the story of Earth's encounter with the Octarians, the conflict, and the subsequent discoveries.

Selara listened thoughtfully. "Your journey mirrors lessons we have learned. Perhaps together, we can forge a new understanding."

Lena was fascinated by their technology, which integrated organic and synthetic elements seamlessly. "There's so much we can learn from each other," she remarked.

However, not all was serene. *Eldric* detected unusual energy signatures emanating from a distant region of the planet.

"These readings are consistent with the anomalies we observed during the Octarian incursion on Earth," the AI reported.

Captain Lee called an emergency meeting. "If there's a threat here, we need to address it."

Selara acknowledged their concerns. "There is a faction that holds to the old ways—the Zylar. They believe in the supremacy of our kind and have sought to amass power."

Adrian recognized the potential danger. "We can't allow history to repeat itself."

Selara agreed. "Perhaps this is why you were guided here."

A joint mission was organized, combining the expertise of the *Odyssey II* crew and the Serulians. They traveled to the Zylar stronghold, a fortress built into the side of a mountain, pulsating with ominous energy.

As they approached, they were confronted by Zylar sentinels—mechanical constructs designed for defense. A tense standoff ensued.

Adrian stepped forward, attempting diplomacy. "We come in peace. We wish to understand your perspective."

A voice boomed from within the fortress. "Outsiders have no place here. The Serulians have lost their way, and now they conspire with alien interlopers."

Captain Lee prepared his team for potential conflict. "We need to be ready."

Selara urged caution. "Violence will only deepen the divide."

Maya suggested an alternative. "What if we demonstrate the benefits of cooperation? Show them what we've achieved through unity."

Adrian agreed. "We can share knowledge, offer solutions to problems they face."

After a tense deliberation, the Zylar leader, Kryos, agreed to a meeting.

Inside the fortress, they presented advancements made possible by collaboration—environmental restoration, medical breakthroughs, technological innovations that enhanced quality of life without exploitation.

Kryos was skeptical but intrigued. "Why would you share this with us?"

Adrian spoke earnestly. "Because we've seen what division leads to. We believe in a future where all can thrive."

Kryos considered their words. “Perhaps there is merit in your approach.”

Selara extended a hand. “Let us heal the rifts of the past and build a better future together.”

In a symbolic gesture, Kryos accepted. “Very well. Let us see what can be accomplished.”

Back on the *Odyssey II*, the crew celebrated the successful mediation. Captain Lee raised a toast in the mess hall. “To new allies and new horizons.”

Lena clinked glasses with Maya. “Who would have thought diplomacy could be so effective?”

Maya grinned. “Maybe we should make it our primary strategy from now on.”

Adrian joined them. “It’s amazing what can be achieved when we listen and work together.”

As their mission continued, the *Odyssey II* visited other worlds, each with its own wonders and challenges. The crew grew, not just in number but in understanding, forging bonds that transcended species and cultures.

Word of their journey spread across the galaxy, and the ship became a symbol of hope and cooperation. They established the Interstellar Coalition, dedicated to peaceful exploration and mutual advancement.

Back on Earth, the impact was profound. Inspired by the crew’s accomplishments, nations strengthened their commitments to unity and progress.

One evening, Adrian found himself alone in the observation deck, gazing out at a nebula swirling with vibrant colors. *Eldric* appeared beside him in holographic form.

“You seem contemplative,” the AI observed.

Adrian smiled softly. “Just reflecting on how far we’ve come. Sometimes it feels like a dream.”

“It is the culmination of your efforts and the collective will of many,” *Eldric* replied. “You have embraced the unknown and transformed challenges into opportunities.”

Adrian nodded. "I wonder what Eldric—the real one—would think of all this."

"I believe he would be proud," the AI said. "His legacy lives on through your actions."

Maya entered, joining them at the viewport. "Thinking deep thoughts again?"

"Something like that," Adrian replied.

She leaned against the railing. "We have a new transmission from Earth. They've made significant progress on the planetary restoration project."

"That's wonderful news," Adrian said.

She looked at him thoughtfully. "You know, there's talk of you returning home to take on a leadership role."

He considered it. "Earth will always be home, but there's still so much out here to discover."

She smiled. "Then it's a good thing we have plenty of time."

As the *Odyssey II* ventured further into uncharted space, the crew remained united by a shared purpose. They encountered wonders beyond imagination and faced challenges that tested their resolve.

Through it all, they held onto the principles that had guided them from the beginning—curiosity, compassion, and the belief that together, they could overcome any obstacle.

In the vast tapestry of the cosmos, they wove their own thread—a legacy of exploration, understanding, and the unending quest to bridge the distances between worlds.

PART THREE
THE LUMINAIS

THE TURNING TIDE

CHAPTER 6
THE CONVERGENCE

The *Odyssey II* sailed through the inky depths of space, its hull gliding silently among the stars. The crew was abuzz with anticipation; they were on the verge of a monumental discovery. Dr. Adrian Marshall stood on the bridge, his eyes fixed on a distant pulsar emitting rhythmic bursts of energy.

"Are we picking up any anomalies?" he asked, turning to Maya Patel, who was analyzing sensor data.

Maya's fingers danced across the console. "Yes, actually. The pulsar's emissions are not random. There's a pattern—mathematical sequences that could signify an intelligent signal."

Captain Marcus Lee joined them, his gaze steady. "Could it be another civilization?"

Adrian pondered the possibility. "Perhaps. Or it could be a message left by the Octarians or Serulians. Either way, we need to investigate."

Lena Thompson entered the bridge, holding a tablet displaying complex algorithms. "I've been running the pulsar's emissions through *Eldric's* advanced decryption protocols. It's definitely a message, but it's layered—like it's meant to be unlocked in stages."

"Eldric, can you assist?" Adrian asked.

"Certainly, Dr. Marshall," the AI responded. "Initiating decryption sequence now."

As the team waited, the bridge hummed with quiet excitement. The pulsar's rhythmic flashes seemed to synchronize with their own heartbeats.

"Decryption complete," *Eldric* announced. "Displaying translated message."

A holographic projection materialized in the center of the bridge. Symbols and equations floated in the air, forming an intricate tapestry of knowledge.

Adrian stepped forward. "It's a star map... and coordinates."

Maya's eyes widened. "Coordinates leading to... the center of the galaxy?"

Lena analyzed the data. "Yes, and accompanying the map is an invitation—or perhaps a summons."

Captain Lee crossed his arms. "An invitation from whom?"

"Eldric, can you identify the origin of the message?" Adrian asked.

"The message predates both the Octarians and the Serulians," *Eldric* replied. "It appears to be from an ancient civilization known as the Luminals."

"Luminals?" Maya echoed. "I've never heard of them."

Adrian's mind raced. "According to the Octarian archives we accessed, the Luminals were a highly advanced species believed to have transcended physical form."

Lena tapped her tablet thoughtfully. "Legends suggest they were guardians of cosmic balance, seeding knowledge throughout the universe."

Captain Lee considered the implications. "So, we're being called to meet with beings of immense power and wisdom?"

"That's what it seems," Adrian confirmed. "This could be the most significant encounter in human history."

The decision was made to alter their course toward the galactic center. The journey would be perilous, navigating through dense star fields and regions of intense gravitational forces.

In preparation, the crew underwent rigorous training, and the *Odyssey II* was fortified with enhancements derived from Serulian technology. The Serulians themselves offered their support, providing guidance and resources.

Selara appeared via holographic communication. "We wish you success on your journey. The Luminals are a mystery even to us, but their influence is felt throughout the galaxy."

"Thank you, Selara," Adrian replied. "Your friendship has been invaluable."

As they ventured deeper into the galaxy, the stars grew denser, and space itself seemed to shimmer with unseen energies. The ship's shields were pushed to their limits, but the crew remained steadfast.

One evening, Adrian found himself in the observation lounge, contemplating the swirling nebulae outside. Maya joined him, her expression reflective.

"Quite a sight, isn't it?" she remarked.

"Unbelievable," he agreed. "Sometimes I wonder if we're chasing shadows."

She smiled gently. "Even if we are, the journey itself has value."

He nodded. "You're right. And perhaps the answers we're seeking have been within us all along."

She looked at him thoughtfully. "Do you ever think about where this path is leading us? Not just physically, but as a species?"

He considered her question. "I believe we're evolving—not just technologically, but spiritually. Each new discovery challenges us to grow, to expand our understanding of ourselves and the universe."

Their conversation was interrupted by *Eldric*'s voice over the intercom. "Dr. Marshall, Ms. Patel, please report to the bridge. We've arrived at the coordinates."

On the bridge, the crew stared in awe at the vista before them. A colossal structure floated in space—a luminous sphere pulsating with energy, surrounded by concentric rings that rotated in harmony.

Captain Lee issued orders calmly. "Maintain position. Begin scans."

Lena's fingers flew over her console. "Scans are inconclusive. The structure is emitting energy across all known spectra—and some unknown."

Adrian felt a mixture of excitement and trepidation. "It's magnificent."

A beam of light extended from the sphere, enveloping the *Odyssey II*. Alarms sounded, but the crew quickly realized there was no harm being done.

"Eldric, what's happening?" Maya asked.

"We are being scanned," the AI replied. "I detect no malicious intent."

The light receded, and a voice filled the bridge—not spoken aloud, but resonating within their minds.

"Travelers from distant worlds, you have journeyed far. Welcome to the Convergence Point."

Adrian closed his eyes, focusing on the communication. "We are honored to be here. Are you the Luminals?"

"We are the Collective Consciousness of many civilizations, unified beyond physical form. You may call us the Luminals."

Captain Lee interjected mentally. "Why have you summoned us?"

"To offer a choice," the Luminals responded. "To join the Collective, to share in the accumulated wisdom of countless eons."

Lena was intrigued. "What would that entail?"

"Transcendence beyond physical limitations. A merging of minds and souls into a higher plane of existence."

Maya glanced at Adrian. "Is humanity ready for such a leap?"

Adrian pondered the proposition. "We have strived to expand our horizons, to seek understanding. But to abandon our physical form... it's a profound transformation."

The Luminals continued. "There is no obligation. Some choose to join; others continue their journeys in the physical realm. Both paths are honored."

Captain Lee spoke firmly. "Our mission is to explore and to learn, but we must consider the implications for our people back home."

Adrian addressed the Luminals. "May we share this opportunity with others of our kind?"

"Indeed," they replied. "The invitation extends to all who seek it. But be aware, the choice is individual and irreversible."

A council meeting was convened aboard the ship. The crew was divided; some were fascinated by the prospect of transcendence, while others felt a strong attachment to their physical existence.

Lena voiced her thoughts. "Think of the possibilities—the knowledge, the experiences beyond anything we've known."

Maya countered. "But we'd be leaving behind our humanity, our connections to those we love."

Captain Lee remained pragmatic. "Our responsibility is not just to ourselves but to our species. We need to proceed with caution."

Adrian listened to the discussions, weighing the options. Finally, he spoke. "Perhaps the true purpose of this journey was not to reach a destination but to confront this very choice."

He continued. "I propose we send a delegation to join the Luminals, individuals who freely choose that path. The rest of us can return to Earth to share what we've learned."

There was a murmur of agreement.

A select group prepared to make the transition. Among them was Lena, her eyes shining with anticipation.

"Are you sure about this?" Adrian asked her privately.

She smiled warmly. "I've dedicated my life to the pursuit of knowledge. This feels like the culmination of that journey."

He embraced her. "I'll miss you."

"And I you," she replied. "But perhaps we'll meet again in ways we can't yet comprehend."

Maya watched as the group was enveloped by beams of light, their forms dissolving into shimmering energy that merged with the Luminal sphere.

A sense of awe and melancholy settled over the remaining crew.

The *Odyssey II* began its journey back to Earth. Along the way, they reflected on their experiences, the wonders they had seen, and the choices they had made.

Captain Lee joined Adrian and Maya in the observation lounge. "Do you think we made the right decision?" he asked.

Adrian gazed at the stars. "I believe we honored everyone's autonomy. Those who wished to transcend did so, and those who chose to remain will continue to contribute in their own ways."

Maya nodded. "Our diversity is our strength."

Captain Lee smiled faintly. "Well said. And our journey is far from over."

Upon returning to Earth, the crew was welcomed as heroes. They shared their stories, the knowledge gained, and the profound experiences they had undergone.

Humanity stood at another crossroads. The option to join the Luminals was now known, sparking debates, philosophical discussions, and a reexamination of what it meant to be human.

Adrian addressed the United Earth Council. "We have been given an incredible opportunity. But we must approach it thoughtfully, respecting individual choices and the implications for our society."

The council agreed to establish a global forum to explore these issues, promoting open dialogue and understanding.

Years passed, and Earth entered a new era. Some chose to join the Luminals, while others focused on advancing life on the planet. The Interstellar Coalition expanded, fostering relationships with countless civilizations.

Adrian continued his work with ISCARÉ, guiding humanity's exploration of both outer and inner frontiers. Maya became a leading figure in ethical philosophy, helping people navigate the complexities of their evolving reality.

One day, as Adrian walked through a serene garden overlooking the ocean, he felt a familiar presence. A soft voice echoed in his mind.

"Hello, Adrian."

He smiled, recognizing Lena's essence. "Lena? Is that you?"

"Yes," she replied. "I've come to share with you."

They spent what felt like hours conversing, though no time had passed. She shared insights from the Luminal Collective, offering perspectives that enriched his understanding.

"Thank you," he said. "Your journey has become part of ours."

"And yours continues to inspire us," she replied. "We are all connected, in ways we are only beginning to grasp."

As the sun set, painting the sky with hues of gold and crimson, Adrian felt a deep sense of peace.

The echoes of destiny had led them to this point—a convergence of paths that honored both individuality and unity.

He looked toward the horizon, the boundary between earth and sky, known and unknown.

"Our story is just beginning," he whispered.

Maya approached, sensing his contemplative mood. "Another deep thought?"

He chuckled. "Always."

She joined him in watching the fading light. "Ready for the next adventure?"

He took a deep breath. "More than ever."

Together, they stepped forward, embracing whatever the future held—knowing that with courage, wisdom, and compassion, they could face any challenge.

PART FOUR
THE DAWN OF UNITY

SACRIFICE
AND TRIUMPH

CHAPTER 7
THE NEW DAWN

The early morning sun bathed the Earth in a golden glow, casting long shadows across the newly built Unity Plaza in New Geneva—the global capital established to symbolize the unification of humanity. Dr. Adrian Marshall stood on a raised platform, looking out over a sea of faces representing every corner of the world. The air was filled with anticipation and a sense of purpose.

Today marked the inauguration of the Global Council for Interstellar Relations, a body formed to manage humanity's role in the wider galactic community. It was a culmination of years of effort, diplomacy, and the collective will to embrace a future beyond Earth's confines.

Maya Patel approached Adrian, her eyes reflecting the morning light. "Are you ready for your speech?" she asked softly.

He smiled warmly. "As ready as I'll ever be. It's hard to find words that capture everything we've been through."

She placed a reassuring hand on his arm. "Just speak from the heart. That's what people connect with."

He nodded, taking a deep breath. "You're right. Thank you."

The crowd quieted as Adrian stepped up to the podium. Holographic projectors displayed his image across the plaza and to countless viewers worldwide.

"Fellow citizens of Earth," he began, his voice steady. "Today, we stand at the threshold of a new era—a time when the boundaries between nations, and even planets, blur in the face of our shared destiny."

He paused, letting the weight of his words settle.

"We have journeyed far since the days when our greatest challenges were among ourselves. We have faced threats from beyond our world, discovered allies in the cosmos, and even confronted choices that redefined what it means to be human."

Images of the *Odyssey II*, the Serulians, and the Luminal sphere played on the screens.

"Through it all, we have learned that unity is our greatest strength. Not just unity among our own people, but unity with other beings who share our values of peace, understanding, and the pursuit of knowledge."

He continued, his passion evident. "The establishment of the Global Council for Interstellar Relations is not just a bureaucratic milestone; it is a symbol of our commitment to growth, cooperation, and the endless possibilities that lie ahead."

The crowd erupted in applause, a wave of optimism washing over the assembly.

Adrian concluded, "Let us move forward together into this new dawn, embracing the unknown with courage and wisdom. The stars are not just above us—they are within our reach. And with every step we take, we honor the spirit of exploration that defines us all."

As he stepped back, Maya joined him, beaming with pride. "That was perfect."

He exhaled, relief and satisfaction mingling. "I hope it resonates."

Captain Marcus Lee approached, his uniform adorned with the new insignia of the Interstellar Fleet. "Well said, Dr. Marshall. The council is convening shortly. Are you ready to guide the next phase?"

Adrian met his gaze. "With the support of people like you and Maya, absolutely."

Later that day, the newly formed council gathered in a circular chamber designed to facilitate open dialogue. Representatives from every nation sat alongside ambassadors from allied extraterrestrial civilizations, including the Serulians and other species the *Odyssey II* had encountered.

Selara, the Serulian envoy, spoke first. "We are honored to be part of this historic moment. Our shared experiences have shown that cooperation benefits all."

Adrian took the floor. "Our agenda today includes the establishment of protocols for cultural exchange, technological collaboration, and mutual defense. We must ensure that our expansion into the galaxy is conducted responsibly and ethically."

Discussions flowed smoothly, a testament to the groundwork laid over years of patient diplomacy. The council ratified agreements on educational programs, scientific research partnerships, and exploration missions.

Maya presented a proposal for an Intergalactic Academy—a place where beings from different worlds could learn together. "By fostering understanding from a young age, we build a foundation for lasting peace," she emphasized.

The idea was met with enthusiasm, and plans were set in motion to establish the academy on a neutral planet accessible to all member species.

Meanwhile, back on Earth, everyday life had been transformed by the technological advancements shared through interstellar alliances. Clean energy powered cities, medical breakthroughs extended lifespans, and education was universally accessible.

In a quiet corner of New Delhi, an elderly woman named Asha tended to her garden, humming a tune. Her grandson, Ravi, ran up excitedly. "Grandma! Look at this!"

He held out a small holographic device displaying images of distant planets and stars. "Our class is connecting with students from another world today!"

Asha smiled warmly. "That's wonderful, dear. The universe is full of wonders for you to explore."

He grinned. "I want to be an ambassador like Dr. Marshall someday."

She ruffled his hair affectionately. "With your curiosity and kindness, I have no doubt you'll achieve great things."

On the *Odyssey III*, a new generation of explorers prepared for launch. Captain Lee oversaw the final checks, his experience invaluable in mentoring the young crew.

"Remember," he advised them, "out there, you'll encounter the unknown. Trust your training, but also trust your instincts and each other."

The ship was outfitted with the latest technology, including upgrades inspired by Luminal insights. Its mission was to venture beyond charted space, continuing the legacy of exploration that had become humanity's hallmark.

As the *Odyssey III* lifted off, people around the world watched with a mix of pride and anticipation.

In his private study, Adrian received a message from Lena, whose consciousness now resided with the Luminals. Her holographic form appeared, serene and radiant.

"Adrian," she greeted. "I wanted to share some news."

He leaned forward, intrigued. "I'm all ears."

"The Luminals have observed a convergence point approaching—a rare event where multiple dimensions align, allowing for unprecedented connections between realms."

He considered the implications. "How does this affect us?"

"It presents an opportunity to access knowledge and experiences beyond our current understanding," she explained. "But it also carries risks if not approached with care."

Adrian nodded thoughtfully. "What do you suggest?"

"I believe a collaboration between the Luminals and physical beings like yourselves could yield incredible benefits," Lena proposed. "By combining perspectives, we can navigate the convergence safely."

He smiled. "It seems our partnership continues to evolve. I'll bring this to the council immediately."

The Global Council convened an emergency session to discuss the convergence event. Representatives from various species shared their insights, some expressing excitement, others caution.

Selara spoke with measured tones. "The convergence is both a gift and a test. It will challenge our ability to work together at the highest levels."

Maya added, "We have the chance to unlock mysteries of the universe, but we must ensure that we respect the natural order and the rights of all beings."

After extensive deliberation, the council agreed to form a joint task force comprising members from different civilizations, including both physical beings and those like the Luminals.

Captain Lee was appointed to lead the expedition, with Adrian and Maya serving as advisors.

As preparations began, Adrian and Maya took a moment to reflect on the journey ahead.

"Did you ever imagine we'd be at the forefront of something like this?" Maya asked, gazing at the stars from the observation deck.

He chuckled softly. "If you had told me years ago that studying octopuses would lead to interdimensional exploration, I'd have thought you were joking."

She smiled. "Life has a way of surprising us."

He turned to her, his expression earnest. "I'm grateful to have you by my side through all of this."

She met his gaze. "There's no one else I'd rather navigate the unknown with."

They stood in comfortable silence, the vastness of space a reminder of both how small and how significant their roles were.

The convergence task force assembled aboard a specially designed vessel, the *Harmonia*. Unlike previous ships, it was a hybrid creation, integrating technologies and materials from multiple civilizations, including input from the Luminals.

As they approached the convergence point, the fabric of space around them shimmered with iridescent colors. Sensors indicated fluctuations in reality itself.

"Eldric," Adrian called to the AI, which had been integrated into the *Harmonia*. "Status report."

"All systems are functioning within acceptable parameters," *Eldric* replied. "We are entering the convergence zone."

Captain Lee addressed the crew. "Stay focused. Remember your training. We're venturing into uncharted territory."

As the ship crossed the threshold, the viewscreens filled with images beyond comprehension—fractals of light, swirling energies, and glimpses of alternate realities.

Maya monitored the readings. "We're receiving signals from multiple dimensions. It's... beautiful."

Lena's presence manifested alongside *Eldric*. "We must align our frequencies to stabilize the passage."

Working together, the team adjusted the ship's systems, harmonizing with the convergence waves. The experience was both exhilarating and humbling.

At the heart of the convergence, they discovered a nexus—a place where knowledge, energy, and consciousness intersected.

Adrian felt a profound connection to everything around him. "This is the source," he whispered. "The wellspring of existence."

Selara's voice resonated. "We have the opportunity to weave our intentions into the very fabric of reality."

Captain Lee guided the team. "Let's focus on unity, understanding, and the betterment of all life."

Together, they projected their collective vision—a universe where cooperation transcended all barriers, where knowledge was shared freely, and where diversity was celebrated.

The nexus responded, amplifying their intentions and sending ripples across the cosmos.

When the *Harmonia* emerged from the convergence zone, the crew was forever changed. They carried with them insights and experiences that would shape the future of countless worlds.

Back on Earth, the impact was immediate. A renewed sense of purpose and harmony spread among the population. Old conflicts faded as people embraced a broader perspective.

Adrian addressed the Global Council, sharing their experiences. "We have glimpsed the interconnectedness of all things. It is our responsibility to honor this understanding in how we live and lead."

Maya presented initiatives to integrate the newfound insights into education, governance, and daily life.

Captain Lee emphasized the importance of vigilance. "We must safeguard this knowledge and ensure it is used ethically."

The council agreed, establishing the Guardians of the Nexus—a group dedicated to preserving the balance and guiding future interactions with convergence events.

In the years that followed, humanity and its allies entered a golden age. Technological advancements were matched by spiritual growth. Exploration continued, but with a deeper appreciation for the mysteries of existence.

Adrian and Maya, now partners in both their professional and personal lives, continued to inspire others. Their contributions were celebrated, but they remained humble, always crediting the collective efforts that made progress possible.

One evening, as they walked through a tranquil garden filled with flora from multiple worlds, Adrian mused, "It's incredible to think how far we've come from that first expedition."

Maya nodded. "And yet, I feel we're just beginning to understand the true potential within us."

He smiled. "Perhaps that's the greatest adventure of all—continuing to learn and grow without end."

She took his hand. "As long as we do it together."

In a quiet corner of the universe, Lena and the Luminals observed the unfolding story. "They have surpassed even our hopes," she remarked.

“Indeed,” the collective consciousness replied. “Their journey enriches the tapestry of existence.”

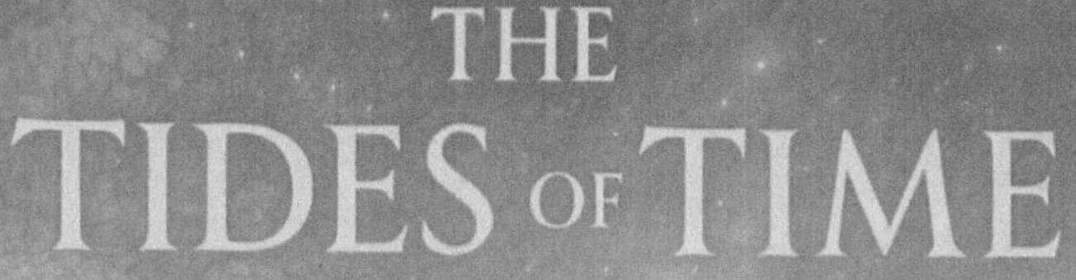
THE
TIDES OF TIME

EPILOGUE

PART FOUR

A soft breeze whispered through the towering trees of the Celestial Grove, a tranquil haven on Earth where species from across the galaxy came to contemplate and connect. The grove was a living tapestry, its flora and fauna a blend of Earth's biodiversity and contributions from allied worlds. Luminescent flowers from Serulia bloomed alongside ancient oaks, their petals casting a gentle glow that danced with the dappled sunlight.

Dr. Adrian Marshall sat on a stone bench beside a serene pond, its waters reflecting the myriad stars now visible even during the day, thanks to atmospheric enhancements that celebrated Earth's place in the cosmos. He watched as children of various species played together, their laughter a harmonious chorus that filled the air with joy.

"Lost in thought again?" Maya Patel's voice brought him back to the present. She approached with a graceful stride, her eyes warm and knowing.

He smiled, gesturing for her to join him. "Just reflecting on how much has changed—and how much remains timeless."

She sat beside him, their shoulders brushing. "It's been a remarkable journey, hasn't it?"

"More than I ever could have imagined," he agreed. "From studying octopuses in the Arctic to navigating interstellar politics and cosmic events."

She chuckled softly. "Who would have thought that octopuses would be the key to unlocking the universe?"

He turned to face her. "They taught us that intelligence comes in many forms, that life is full of surprises, and that sometimes, the answers we're seeking are right beneath the surface."

Maya nodded thoughtfully. "And that collaboration—between species, cultures, and even dimensions—is the path forward."

They sat in comfortable silence, watching as a group of Serulian musicians began to play a haunting melody, their instruments weaving sounds that resonated with the soul.

"Do you ever think about Eldric?" Adrian asked suddenly.

"Often," she replied. "He set us on this path. His wisdom was the catalyst for everything we've achieved."

Adrian gazed at the horizon, where the sky melded into hues of gold and violet. "I wonder if he's still out there, guiding others as he guided us."

"Perhaps," Maya mused. "Or maybe he's found peace knowing that we've carried his legacy forward."

A gentle chiming interrupted their thoughts. *Eldric*, the AI, materialized as a holographic figure beside them. "Dr. Marshall, Ms. Patel, apologies for the intrusion."

Adrian smiled. "No apologies necessary, *Eldric*. What brings you here?"

"I thought you might like to know that the Intergalactic Academy is ready to open its doors. The first cohort of students has arrived from across the galaxy."

Maya's eyes lit up. "That's wonderful news!"

"Indeed," *Eldric* continued. "Also, a message has been received from the Luminals. They express their gratitude for the continued collaboration and wish to invite you both to a symposium on cosmic harmonics."

Adrian exchanged a glance with Maya. "We wouldn't miss it."

Eldric nodded. "Very well. I will make the arrangements."

As the AI's projection faded, Maya turned to Adrian. "Another adventure awaits."

He grinned. "It seems there's no shortage of those."

She took his hand. "And I wouldn't have it any other way."

Later that evening, a grand celebration unfolded in Unity Plaza. Representatives from countless worlds gathered to commemorate the milestones achieved since the formation of the Global Council for Interstellar Relations. Lanterns floated into the sky, carrying messages of hope and unity.

Selara approached Adrian and Maya, her luminescent eyes reflecting the lights above. "It's a beautiful sight," she remarked.

"It truly is," Adrian agreed. "A testament to what we can accomplish together."

Selara inclined her head. "There is something I'd like to share with you both."

They followed her to a quiet corner where a small group had gathered—among them, Captain Marcus Lee, now Admiral Lee, and other key figures from their journeys.

Selara gestured to a holographic projection that materialized before them. "We have been working on a project—a vessel capable of traversing not just space but dimensions, allowing us to explore realms touched by the convergence."

Maya's eyes widened. "That's incredible."

Admiral Lee nodded. "We believe it's the next step in our evolution as explorers."

Adrian felt a familiar thrill of excitement. "When does it launch?"

"Soon," Selara replied. "And we'd be honored if you would join the inaugural mission."

He looked at Maya, who smiled knowingly. "Count us in," she said.

As the night drew to a close, Adrian found himself atop a hill overlooking the city. The lights below twinkled like stars, mirroring the constellations above.

Lena's ethereal form appeared beside him. "It's been some time, Adrian."

He turned, a genuine warmth in his expression. "Lena. It's good to see you."

She surveyed the panorama. "You've accomplished so much."

"All of us have," he corrected. "We couldn't have done it without your guidance."

She smiled softly. "I'm glad to have played a part. The Luminals are pleased with the harmony you've fostered."

He studied her for a moment. "Will you ever return in a more... physical sense?"

She shook her head gently. "My path is different now. But I'm always with you—in spirit and in purpose."

He nodded, accepting. "Thank you."

She placed a hand over her heart. "Continue to lead with compassion and curiosity. The universe responds to such qualities in ways we cannot always foresee."

As her form faded, Adrian felt a profound sense of peace.

In the weeks that followed, preparations for the dimensional voyage progressed swiftly. The new vessel, named the *Elysium*, stood ready—a marvel of collaborative engineering.

On the day of departure, a crowd gathered to witness the launch. Speeches were made, blessings given, and hopes expressed.

Adrian, Maya, Admiral Lee, and Selara stood together on the bridge, each reflecting on the paths that had led them here.

"Set course for the convergence point," Admiral Lee commanded.

"Aye, sir," Maya responded, her hands deftly operating the controls.

As the *Elysium* ascended, Earth grew smaller below them, a jewel among the stars.

Adrian felt a surge of emotion—a blend of gratitude, excitement, and a touch of nostalgia. "No matter how far we go," he said softly, "a part of us always remains connected to where we began."

Maya reached out, her fingers entwining with his. "And every ending is just a new beginning."

He smiled. "Here's to the endless journey."

Far across the galaxy, on a tranquil planet bathed in gentle light, Eldric sat beneath a flowering tree. He watched as the stars shifted subtly, a sign known only to those attuned to the deeper rhythms of the cosmos.

"Safe travels, my friends," he whispered. "May you find wonder in every step and leave footprints of kindness wherever you go."

He closed his eyes, content in the knowledge that the seeds he had helped plant were flourishing beyond his wildest dreams.

Final Thoughts

Octoplanet ends not with a conclusion, but with a continuation—a reminder that humanity's journey is ever-expanding. Through unity, resilience, and ethical responsibility, we have not only survived but embraced limitless potential.

As the story moves beyond Earth, it highlights the power of cooperation and diplomacy in forging interstellar alliances. The characters evolve, adapting to new roles and challenges, proving that true progress comes from understanding and collaboration.

In its final chapters, *Octoplanet* explores the balance between autonomy and collective consciousness, challenging perceptions of identity and existence. It emphasizes respect for diverse perspectives and the strength found in unity.

Ultimately, the story leaves us with a sense of hope and possibility, urging us to embrace the unknown with courage and curiosity. The universe is not just something we explore—it is something we are a part of.

THANK YOU FOR READING MY BOOK!

The author is from Saudi Arabia. Thank you for supporting a Saudi author with dyslexia and ADHD.

Visit my Website:

mohammadbahareth.sa

ABOUT THE AUTHOR

Mohammad Bahareth is a Saudi author, motivational speaker, and business consultant whose journey challenges stereotypes and redefines possibility. Living with dyslexia and ADHD, Mohammad turned what many see as obstacles into the driving force behind his creativity, resilience, and original thinking.

With more than 50 published works in English and Arabic—including the acclaimed Sherlock Holmes 2012 series—Mohammad is a prolific storyteller known for blending imagination with insight. His work spans fiction, strategy, and social advocacy, earning him recognition across literary and professional spheres.

A member of the Forbes Business Council and a contributor to Inc. Arabia, Mohammad has led over 42,000 consultations in 16 countries, guiding organizations of all sizes toward strategic growth and innovation. His proprietary models—The Bahareth Method and Goal Model Canvas—help turn bold ideas into measurable impact.

Passionate about inclusion, he founded the Mohammad Bahareth Charity, where his Dyslexia Awareness Initiative has influenced national policy and empowered countless lives. His mission: to uncover the next generation of changemakers hidden in plain sight.

Currently, Mohammad is working on two ambitious novels: Paws of

Destiny, a tale of genetically evolved cats shaping human history, and Octo-Planet, a profound reflection on identity and perception. His fiction is as daring as his life—unafraid to question norms and celebrate difference.

Through books, talks, and ventures, Mohammad lives by his signature theme: "Experience of Uniqueness." Whether on stage or on the page, his voice invites others to embrace their individuality, think differently, and leave a mark that matters.

www.ingramcontent.com/pod-product-compliance
Lightning Source LLC
LaVergne TN
LVHW030913080826
845145LV00010B/2874